They don't understand. . . .

Lauren was practically jumping out of her gym shoes. "You mean Heidi's going to be in a big meet, right here in Denver?! So soon?"

"The biggest," said Dimitri.

"You'll be super," Darlene said confidently. "I've been watching you work out. You're as good as anybody."

"You haven't seen anybody," I snapped.

I lowered my eyes. I would apologize to Darlene, but it was the truth. Darlene and the rest of the Pinecones were terrific kids, but they didn't know anything about the real world of competition. At the level Dimitri was talking about, it's cutthroat.

I was afraid.

**Look for these and other books
in THE GYMNASTS series:**

THE GYMNASTS

#19 TOUGH AT THE TOP

Elizabeth Levy

AN
APPLE
PAPERBACK

SCHOLASTIC INC.
New York Toronto London Auckland Sydney

ISBN 0-590-44694-0

12 11 10 9 8 7 6 5 4 3 2 1   1 2 3 4 5 6/9

Printed in the U.S.A.   40

First Scholastic printing, September 1991

To all my pen pals.

TOUGH AT THE TOP

Change

I looked at myself in the mirror and flexed my bicep. It bounced up like a rubber ball. I laughed. I've been lifting weights for the past six months. Some of the muscles and *all* of the laughing are new.

I used to cry when I saw myself in the mirror. I still weigh myself every day. I can't help that.

"Heidi!" shouted my mother. "What are you doing in there?"

My mother doesn't like closed doors.

"I'll be out in a minute," I said. I wished my brother, Chris, were home. It's easier on me when he's around, but he wasn't. He's a champion freestyle skier who goes to school and trains in Lake Placid.

1

I put on a pair of tights and a Bronco sweat-shirt that my friend Darlene gave me. Darlene is always after me to wear bright colors, and what could be brighter than Bronco Orange?

Darlene's dad is a football star on the Denver Broncos. I never used to have time to follow football. Now, I love it.

"Heidi!" my mom called again. "Please come down and have breakfast."

Mom has a way of saying "please" that sets my teeth on edge. It always sounds as if I've already disobeyed her. I realize the past year or so of my life hasn't been easy for her, either. Still, I wish she'd learn to relax.

I opened my door. Mom was waiting just outside. She frowned when she saw me.

"That sweatshirt is so big on you, it makes you look . . . " Mom paused. I knew Mom didn't want to tell me I looked fat. I used to be obsessed with my weight.

"Gross?" I asked, teasing her.

Mom gave me a puzzled look. She doesn't take well to teasing.

"No, no," said Mom quickly. "Sloppy. Sloppy was the word I was looking for. You have such nice clothes — you should wear them."

"Relax, Mom," I said. "I've got a new leotard on underneath. I'll show it off at the gym."

Mom sniffed but didn't say anything. I knew

she was trying hard not to make a sarcastic crack about the place where I work out, the Evergreen Gymnastics Academy. It may sound fancy, but it's not, and it's a big comedown from the glamourous gym in California where Mom had taken me for four years, up until last year.

I went into the breakfast room and started to eat a bowl of oatmeal and raisins. I counted the raisins. It's a bad habit left over from the time when I used to count everything I ate.

My dad saw me doing it and frowned, but he didn't say anything. Dad lets Mom "handle" me. He doesn't like to talk about the time I was sick.

I started gymnastics when I was in kindergarten, and right away I was good. My whole family is athletic. Mom was a ballet dancer. Dad is a fantastic golfer.

I was five years old when my first gymnastics coach told my parents that I had the strength and coordination to be really excellent. I knew I could do things that other kids couldn't. I also hated to lose.

When you're naturally talented in gymnastics — and just starting out — it's easy. I had no trouble beating other kids. But then the higher I got in competition, the more I discovered how many great gymnasts there are in the world. It was tough enough getting to be one of the best in the United States. Then I went to my first international competition in Japan. I scored eighteenth out of twenty. And I did the best of all the Americans at that competition.

I'm naturally thin, but my coach out in California wanted me to lose a few pounds. She kept telling me that the international judges looked for "sleek." Whenever I looked in the mirror, I just didn't "see" sleek. I started making myself throw up after I ate one little french fry.

My California coach didn't know. She was happy that I was so tiny. I looked nine years old, not fourteen.

Japan was my first and last big international competition. When I got back to California I got a cold, and it turned into bronchitis. The doctors told my mom that I was seriously malnourished. I had to come back to our hometown, Denver, and I was admitted to Children's Hospital.

I cried all the way home on the plane from California to Denver. The flight attendant thought that somebody in my family had just died. No one had, but I thought that everything I'd worked so hard for was about to go up in smoke. I was sure that if I didn't train for even a week, I'd be so out of shape that my coach would never take me back.

I dreaded coming back to Denver and going into the hospital. I thought it was the end of gymnastics for me. I lay in the hospital bed and had to think about things that I'd never had time for before. All the doctors told me I had to change — that my eating habits were killing me. I had read about bulemic and anorexic kids, but I thought that because I was still so muscular, it couldn't be me. The doctors told me I was wrong.

I didn't want to go back to California. I thought about quitting gymnastics altogether.

Then I met the Pinecones. They're good gymnasts, but not great ones. They're happy if they can just beat the local team that they hate. But they have a lot of fun. They laugh a lot, and they like one another. They don't think the fate of the world depends on learning a new trick. I hadn't hung out with kids like them since I was little.

Everyone who knows anything about gymnastics can't believe that I'm not with a bigger club. I don't care. The Pinecones make gymnastics fun for me again. I haven't regretted it yet.

It Doesn't Make Sense

Mom hates the Pinecones, and she hates the Evergreen Gymnastics Academy. Mom thinks the Pinecones are strictly amateurs.

I'm in therapy now with a psychologist. I call Dr. Joe, "my shrink." He says he doesn't care what I call him as long as I keep coming to see him. He thinks the Pinecones are good for me. In fact, he doesn't think it's a bad thing that Mom hates them. He says change is hard on everybody. I don't always understand exactly what he means.

Mom comes from a very wealthy family on the East Coast. Even though a lot of people in Denver are hurting for money, my parents aren't. It's a good thing, because it takes a lot of money to train at my level.

I like Saturdays. The Pinecones come to the gym on Saturday mornings. Weekdays can be lonely. I have the gym to myself until the other kids come in after school. I don't go to school. I take correspondence courses and have a private tutor so I'll have the time to practice. I know that if I'm really going to make a comeback, I'll have to push myself.

Mom drove up to the gym, which is an old warehouse behind a shopping mall — not exactly the height of glamour. She parked the car.

"You don't have to come in with me," I said. I might have snapped, although I didn't mean to. Sometimes I sound mean to my mom even when I don't have a reason.

Mom looked hurt, although she knows I don't like her to watch me practice. One of the things I love about the Evergreen Gym is that the owner and one of the coaches, Patrick Harmon, doesn't allow the parents to watch.

"Dimitri asked that I come in and talk to him and Patrick," said Mom.

Dimitri Vickorskoff has made all the difference in my comeback, but for some reason Mom doesn't trust him. Dimitri immigrated to the United States from Hungary just last year. He came to Denver by chance, although I have a sneaking feeling that he wound up at the Evergreen Gymnastics Academy because he knew I had been trying for my comeback there.

Dimitri and Patrick have been coaching me together. Patrick is great for my confidence. He's young and full of enthusiasm. He thinks everything's possible. Dimitri is older, and he coached two Olympic gold medalists. There are almost a dozen tricks in gymnastics Dimitri invented and that are called the Vickorskoff Twist, or the Vickorskoff Vault. Dimitri is great for my technique. He knows the international gymnastics world better than anybody, and when it's time for me to compete again, I'll be glad that he's on my side.

I wondered why Dimitri had asked to talk to my mother. Usually Dimitri doesn't waste his time talking to parents. He likes to deal with the gymnasts directly.

I got out of the passenger seat and carefully closed the door.

Two of my favorite Pinecones, Darlene Broderick and Cindi Jockett, were just driving up. Darlene's dad was driving. His football nickname is "Big Beef," and it's no exaggeration. He's huge, and he's got a booming laugh.

I'm not impressed with celebrities. I've been treated like one myself. But I like Darlene's dad. He waved to us and got out of his car.

"Heidi Clare!" said Big Beef.

"Big Beef," said Cindi, "you know her name's Heidi Ferguson."

"Hei-di Clare, it's good to see you," said Big Beef.

I gave him a weak smile.

"Dad, that's an A-plus groaner," moaned Darlene, shaking her head. "Heidi's heard all the Heidi puns that you can come up with."

"Let Hei-di-cide if she doesn't like my jokes," said Big Beef. He winked at me.

I started to giggle. It was hard not to like a grown man who weighs 260 pounds and makes up puns.

"Heidi's name is not a joke," said Mom.

Big Beef didn't shrink the way most people do when Mom puts on her "cold" voice.

"Heidi," he asked in a normal voice, "did I hurt your feelings?"

"No, Mr. Broderick," I said.

"You can call me 'Hamburger.' "

Darlene sighed. "Dad, enough's enough. It's bad *enough* that you're coming inside today. You don't have to take over with your jokes."

"Patrick and Dimitri asked to meet with me," said Big Beef. "Otherwise I might consider sleeping on a Saturday morning."

"That's a relief," I whispered. Cindi heard me.

"What's a relief?" she asked.

"I'm just glad that my mom wasn't the only one called in for a meeting," I said.

We went into the locker room. Several other

gymnasts were already there. Lauren Baca, another of my favorites, was already dressed in her leotard.

"Something's going on," said Lauren.

"What do you mean?" asked Cindi.

"Patrick and Dimitri are having a big meeting with some strangers," said Lauren. "And then they called last night and asked my mom to come in this morning." Lauren's mom is a politician. She was elected to the city council, and Lauren thinks that her mom wants to be mayor of Denver one day.

"They called all of our parents," said Darlene.

"Uh-uhh," said Ti An Truong, who's only nine. "They didn't call mine."

"Not mine, either," said Ashley Frank, another one of the younger Pinecones. We polled the kids in the locker room. The only parents who had been called in were Darlene's, Lauren's, and mine.

"I don't get it," said Jodi Sutton. "You kids aren't in trouble."

Jodi's a good kid and a good gymnast, but somehow or other she *is* the one who usually gets in trouble.

"I don't know what it is," said Lauren, "but Patrick looks pretty nervous."

"It doesn't make sense," I said.

Wild Card

You have to see Dimitri to believe him. He's as tall as Big Beef, and he's got a big face with a big moustache. Everything about Dimitri seems oversized, and everything about him is emotional.

Patrick is half Dimitri's age, but Patrick's the calm one. Sometimes I think that nothing can ruffle him. Patrick seems quiet to me, and then he laughs. He's got a big laugh, and my mother doesn't like him. She thinks he's too young to be coaching someone like me, and she thinks that Dimitri is too excitable. I say they make a good team.

Dimitri was deep in conversation with Big Beef and Lauren's mom. My mom was standing just a little bit outside of the circle with her arms across her chest.

Patrick saw us come out of the locker room and waved. "Heidi, come over here. We have tremendously exciting news."

"I bet you're going to be on TV," said Ti An.

"Maybe they want Heidi to swing from the rafters at City Hall," said Jodi.

"That's silly," I said. "It's probably nothing." The Pinecones all followed me over to the adults. Dimitri was gesturing wildly with his hands. He swung his right hand out and almost bopped me on the nose.

"Hei-dee!" shouted Dimitri. "Vait till you hear!" Dimitri's English has gotten better, but when he's excited, which is most of the time, his accent gets thicker and thicker.

Mom was chewing on her lip. I could tell that whatever the news was she didn't like it.

"What?" I asked.

"It's a *coup*!" said Dimitri.

"A coo?" I repeated. I didn't know what he was talking about.

"What Dimitri's trying to say," said Patrick with a huge grin on his face, "is that Dimitri's pulled off quite a *coup* for Denver. He has convinced the Association of International Gymnasts to hold a Challenge Cup right here in Denver."

"I didn't vant to tell you sooner," exploded Dimitri. "I didn't know if it vould happen. They vere going to have in Budapest, but now Budapest has no money, so I say, 'Vait, I'm here now. In America. Denver perfect city.' "

"That's why he wanted to talk to me," said Lauren's mom. "I'm sure I can get the city council to declare October twenty-eighth 'Denver's Salute to Gymnastics.' "

"And I'm going to ask the Broncos' promotion department to help," said Big Beef. "It's going to be held in the same arena where the Denver Nuggets basketball team plays. We often do joint promotions for the city."

"Hold it, hold it," I said, turning and facing Patrick. "Did I hear the twenty-eighth of October?"

"I know that gives us just a little over a month to train, but you're strong," said Patrick. "Dimitri thinks you're ready."

I shook my head. "Whoa, this wasn't planned. Dimitri, we were talking about maybe *six* months from now I'd try for a comeback, but . . . "

Mom was nodding her head up and down, but Dimitri was shaking his just as vigorously.

Lauren was practically jumping out of her gym

shoes. "You mean Heidi's going to be in a big meet, right here in Denver?! So soon?"

"The biggest," said Dimitri. "The best gymnasts from all over the vorld."

"Dimitri," I said, "I haven't competed for one year. No way will I be invited to this meet. I know these Challenge Cups. I haven't scored high in the past year at an international event."

"No, no," said Dimitri. "I already talk to the officials. I tell them hometown should have a vild cold."

"A vile cold?"

"I think he means a wild card," said Patrick.

"Count me out," I said. "It's too soon."

Darlene interrupted. "You'll be super," she said confidently. "I've been watching you work out. You're as good as anybody."

"You haven't seen anybody," I snapped.

Darlene backed off. I knew I had hurt her feelings, and I was sorry, but it was the truth. Darlene and the rest of the Pinecones were terrific kids, but they didn't know anything about the real world of competition. At the level Dimitri was talking about, it's cutthroat.

Big Beef put his arm around Darlene's shoulders and kept looking at me. I lowered my eyes. I would apologize to Darlene, but I had a feeling that Big Beef, because he plays in professional sports, knew what I was feeling. I was afraid.

Dimitri, in typical Dimitri style, just pretended that I hadn't objected at all. "No, no . . . ve fine-tune — everything's ready. You're stronger than even before. Ve show them a new Heidi Ferguson."

"Dimitri," I protested, "read my lips. You're not going to show them any Heidi Ferguson. I can't go into big competition when I'm not prepared. I'll fall on my face."

Dimitri frowned. "No, no falls," he said. "Ve practice, practice. You do routine in sleep. No falls."

"It's an expression, Dimitri," I said, exasperated. "It means I'll fall flat."

Dimitri still frowned. He grabbed my arm and felt my muscle. "No flat . . . firm, good. You strong."

Mom has opinions on practically everything, especially if it has to do with my career, but she had been strangely silent during this discussion.

"Heidi's still fragile," she said finally.

Now it was Patrick's turn to frown. "Maybe before when she was too thin. She looks better now than she ever did."

"Patrick's right," said Dimitri. "Tiny is old shoe in gymnastics. Judges look for something new. You vill be the divverent." Dimitri put his arm around me.

"I'm strong," I admitted. "But I'm not prepared."

"You're ready!" said Patrick. "Trust us."

"Patrick," said my mother in her most obnoxious voice, "Heidi knows what she's capable of better than you do."

Patrick looked at me and smiled. He's got a warm, great smile. "Heidi, maybe we sprang it on you too fast. You don't have to make your mind up right away."

"Hey, wait a minute," said Big Beef. "I have to tell the Bronco promotion department if we're doing it."

"Oh, ve're going to hold the meet," said Dimitri. "Heidi vill be there."

"No, Dimitri," said Patrick, and he doesn't usually contradict Dimitri. "It's Heidi's decision. If Heidi says that she's not ready, she's not ready."

"Good," said my mother. "Heidi and I have made her decision. You should have consulted me before making all this hullabaloo."

"The meet is going on whether Heidi participates or not," said Patrick.

"She has made up her mind," said my mother forcefully.

"Hey," whispered Lauren. "You haven't really made up your mind that you don't want to do it, have you?"

Lauren looked so anxious. I was grateful to her. Lauren was right. I wasn't sure what I wanted to do, but I didn't want Mom to decide for me.

"No, she *hasn't* made up her mind," I said loudly. I hate being discussed in the third person, anyway.

The Pinecones cheered.

4

Nothing to Prove

The next day I warmed up with some slow stretches. The Pinecones couldn't stop chattering about the news of the Challenge Cup.

"What are you going to do?" Ti An asked. "Please tell me. I can't stand not knowing." Ti An doesn't like suspense. She hates scary movies.

"Ti An," I said, "I don't know."

"She's gonna do it," Cindi said confidently.

I shook my head and sighed. "Look, guys, don't push me on this. You don't understand what's involved."

Cindi made a face. "Come off it, Heidi. You sound like a dorky grown-up."

I made a face.

Cindi put her hands on her hips. "Don't make a face at me," she said.

18

I started to get angry and then I stopped myself. Nobody can say that the Pinecones treat me with kid gloves. That's why I like them.

"I honestly don't know what to do, okay?"

"What do you have to lose?" asked Lauren. "You know you're good. And if you want to have any chance to go to the Olympics, you've got to show people that you're back."

"You've got no idea what the competition's like, Lauren. The new Chinese girls are incredible. They're ferocious and fearless, and don't think that the Russians have fallen just because the cold war is over. They're tigers. They'll do anything to win."

"You make them sound like something from a *National Geographic* special," said Jodi. "They're just human."

"Ha!" I said. I finished my warm-ups.

"So what have you decided?" asked Ti An again.

"Ti An, cool it," I said. "I *don't* know."

"I still think you should do it," said Darlene. "My dad says that when you're afraid of failing at something, it's a hint from your gut that you should go for it."

"Thank you for the inspirational advice," I said. "I don't need hints from my gut. This is just going to be a practical decision. I may not be ready yet."

After my warm-ups, I put on my sweatband and went to the new weight room that Dimitri had talked Patrick into getting.

Dimitri had devised a program for me that emphasized upper-body strength. I start out on the machines, but then I spend most of my time using "free weights," which are just a fancier name for dumbbells.

Instead of using heavy weights, I do lots of repetitions with light weights. When we're using three- to five-pound weights we don't have to have a coach spotting us. It's kind of boring, so when I heard somebody come into the room I was glad to take a break.

Then I saw who it was. Becky Dyson is a good gymnast. But I've met lots of good gymnasts, and Becky isn't *that* good. Unfortunately, she thinks she *is*. When I started working out at the gym, she immediately assumed that she and I would be best friends. I don't have best friends. It's just not something I do. If that hurts people's feelings, too bad.

Becky picked up a two-pound weight. She nodded hello.

"I hear you told Dimitri to take his Challenge Cup and shove it," said Becky. The rumor wires in our gym move faster than a track star on steroids.

"Where did you hear that?" I asked.

"They say that Dimitri's really upset that you're not doing it," said Becky, not really answering my question.

I hate it when anybody tells me "they say."

"I can't talk right now," I grunted. It's impossible to do the weights correctly and still have breath left to talk. I did my twelve repetitions and then rested.

Becky somehow was able to talk while she worked out. I knew it meant that she wasn't really concentrating, but I'm not her coach.

I got up and put my weights back on the rack.

"I'm glad you've bent Dimitri's nose out of joint," said Becky. "Everybody around here thinks Dimitri's some gymnastics god or something."

I was all sweaty. I stuck out my lip and blew my bangs out of my face.

One thing Becky is *not* good at is reading other people's minds. She didn't seem to have a clue that I didn't want to talk.

"Anyhow, I just wanted you to know that I don't think you're chicken."

"Thanks, Becky," I said sarcastically. "I'm not worried about it." I don't have to prove anything to anybody. That's been the whole point of my therapy.

So if I had nothing to prove, why didn't I feel good? In my gut, as Big Beef would say, I had a lot of questions.

5

It's a Big Vorld

Dimitri was waiting for me by the beam. I knew that I was going to have to face him sooner or later. I had heard rumors before I started to work with him that he had a terrible temper, but he hadn't shown it to me. Now I wondered if it was going to be my turn.

Dimitri loves gadgets and high tech. He had a computer printout of my beam routine. "Today, ve add a little flair — something secret to surprise them vith — you so strong you use beam like the men use the pommel horse. It's different."

I stared at him. I couldn't believe that he wasn't going to discuss the Challenge Cup with me.

"Dimitri," I said, "we just can't start working as if nothing happened."

"Vot happened?" Dimitri asked, sounding anxious. "You didn't hurt yourself vith veights?"

"No, no," I said quickly. "But we should talk about the Challenge Cup. I don't think I'm ready. I think it's too soon."

Dimitri shrugged. He patted the beam. "No talk. Ve vork out. Then talk."

If I had disagreed with my coach in California about an appearance at a meet she had arranged, I would have been screamed at as an ungrateful, stupid brat.

"Dimitri . . ." I stuttered.

"Vork . . . then talk."

I just shook my head. I was sure that Dimitri was trying a clever bit of reverse psychology.

My beam routine starts relatively simply. Dimitri doesn't believe in risky mounts to the beam.

"Okay," said Dimitri. *Okay* was one of the first words he learned in English, and he used it all the time. "Now, you're up, and the judges, they have settled down to concentrate on you. Now ve spectacular them."

"Spectacular them?" I couldn't help giggling. Dimitri grinned at me. Sometimes I think he makes fun of his own English. Even when I'm standing on the beam, Dimitri is so tall that it feels as if he's at eye level.

"You mean put in a risky move," I said.

"No, not so risky, but looks risky." Dimitri's hands flew through the air as he showed me what he wanted me to do. His hands are so expressive that I could see my body doing what he described.

I would dive for the beam in a leap with my chest out. It would look like a suicide move, as if I were falling, but because of my new arm strength, I'd catch all my weight with my hands and immediately flair my legs out to either side of the beam. It's a move first done by Kurt Thomas on the men's pommel horse.

I tried it. Once I got the right rhythm the move was actually not as hard as it looked.

"Qvick! Qvick!" shouted Dimitri. "The faster the legs go it looks better, but easy."

Dimitri was right. The momentum of my legs lifted weight off my arms. Dimitri grinned at me.

"Beautiful, no?"

I stopped and rested on the beam. I grinned at him. "It's neat," I admitted. "I've never seen any girl do this before."

"No von else does this," said Dimitri. "They'll name it the Ferguson Flair. I promise."

"Not the Vickerskoff?" I teased.

Dimitri shook his head. "Already too many

things named after me. This is new. For you. Do it again."

"Von more time," I heard Lauren say behind me. When Dimitri says "von more time," it means that you're going to be doing it at least a dozen more times. Dimitri doesn't know the meaning of the words "I'm tired."

I hadn't realized that the Pinecones were watching me. To me, the best moments in gymnastics are when I'm working so hard that I don't notice anything around me.

Patrick gave a thumbs-up sign to Dimitri. I looked over at him. "Dimitri and I had been working out that new move, and I wanted to see how it flew," said Patrick. "Okay, girls, let's get back over to the vault."

"It's beautiful," said Darlene to me over her shoulder.

I licked my lips. I love learning new tricks. It's fun to try something that nobody's done before. It's an incredible kick.

I did the new move, again and again. Each time I did it, I got my legs higher and higher. Finally, by the twelfth time, my arms were shaking from the effort.

"Von more time!" sang out Dimitri.

I shook my head. "I'm bushed," I told him.

"Honest . . . vonce more. Then ve stop."

"Dimitri, I'm tired," I said.

"Sure you are," said Dimitri. Sometimes his English is perfect.

I swallowed hard.

"Okay," I grunted. I pushed myself and stood up on the beam. I did my leap and then dived for the beam. My hands caught the beam a split second before I would have hit it with my chest. My forearms tingled from the impact, but I swung my legs out. Sweat was dripping down my forehead.

"Point toes! Point toes!" Dimitri screamed at me.

I just grunted and tried to point my toes. Then I completed the move. I was physically spent. I didn't have "von more time" in me.

"Gooood," said Dimitri. He squeezed my shoulder. "It's goood, no?"

"Yes," I had to admit. I can tell right away when a new trick suits me, and this one did.

Dimitri grinned at me. "Tomorrow! Ve add just a little twist. You push up so legs go first von side of beam, then the other. Not so much hard! Judges never seen anything like it! Ve must be quick."

"There really isn't anybody else in the world doing this?" I asked him again.

"No, no." Dimitri shook his head.

"Did you come up with this just to whet my

appetite to show it off at the Challenge Cup?" I asked Dimitri.

"Vots vet appetite?" asked Dimitri. "You thirsty?"

"Come off it, Dimitri," I said. "I know you want me to do this for the Challenge Cup."

"It very good for the Challenge Cup. Nobody do it *now*, but who knows?" Dimitri widened his eyes so that he looked innocent. "You know, it's a big vorld, and somebody else might think of it."

I didn't want anybody else showing off my new move but me.

 **6**

Sitting on a Fence Hurts

"So Dimitri's teaching me this new move that he and Patrick thought up, and *I* know he wants me to do it at the Challenge Cup, but he won't admit it."

Dr. Joe had his feet up, and I sat opposite him. When I go to see him I don't lie on a couch or anything like that. Dr. Joe is short, and he reminds me a little of Patrick. They don't really look alike — Dr. Joe's got dark brown hair and a mustache — but they both go straight to the heart of the matter.

"Is the move fun?" Dr. Joe asked me.

The question surprised me. I nodded. My mom would never think of asking if a move was fun or not. She'd only want to know if it was (a) dangerous, and (b) something that would impress the judges.

I sat back and didn't look at Dr. Joe. He's got lots of other things to look at in his office. I watched the fish swimming around in his fish tank.

"Mom doesn't want me to do the Challenge Cup," I said. "I'm not sure how much she wants me to make a comeback."

"She's probably ambivalent," said Dr. Joe. "Do you know what that means? It means she's got conflicting feelings. But let's not talk about her for a minute. What about you?"

"What about me?" I asked. There's a crystal castle in the fish tank and bubbles come up through it to the top. Dr. Joe waited. He didn't repeat the question.

"I don't know what I want," I said. "Suppose I enter the Challenge Cup and I'm really lousy. That would about finish my chances for the Olympics in 1992."

Dr. Joe just kept quiet.

"Of course, if I don't start competing soon, I'll have *no* chance to go to the Olympics," I continued. "Why do those bubbles come out of the castle?"

"I like the way it looks," said Dr. Joe. "It's got

a hose under the sand. I have to clean it regularly. I guess you know what it feels like to be ambivalent."

"What do you think I should do?" I asked.

"I honestly don't know," he said.

"I think you think I should go for it," I insisted.

Dr. Joe put his feet on the floor and sat forward. "Heidi, when you're out there performing, it's not me or your mother or father. It's you alone. So nobody can make that decision for you."

"I think Mom feels guilty that she pushed me into competing and then I got sick. I think she *wants* me to quit."

"She's scared for you," said Dr. Joe. "That's human. But you and I know that it wasn't gymnastics that was the problem. It was thinking that you had to be perfect and wanting to control every part of your life. Plenty of girls who aren't world-class gymnasts are bulemic or have anorexia."

"Plenty of gymnasts are," I said.

"Heidi," said Dr. Joe, "we've talked about this before. Gymnastics gives you great joy, but it has also brought you great anxiety. Only you can tell whether the joy outweighs the anxiety."

"So you *do* want me to enter the Challenge Cup?" I asked.

Dr. Joe leaned back and put his feet up on the

ottoman. "You know what the problem is with fences?" he asked.

"Is this a riddle?" I demanded.

Dr. Joe put his hands behind his head and stretched. "Fences hurt like the dickens when you're sitting on one," he said.

"Very funny," I muttered.

"I wasn't joking," said Dr. Joe.

Set Them on Their Noses

"I can't believe we get to be in the Challenge Cup," said Lauren. "I'm so excited!" When Lauren's excited her voice goes up an octave. I had just finished my workout as the Pinecones and other kids were arriving after school.

I stared at Lauren. "I still haven't made up my mind yet," I said to her.

"I know," said Lauren, "but we're going to be the volunteers. We get to march the gymnasts around, don't we, Patrick?"

Patrick put down his clipboard. He had a piece of paper in his hand. "Absolutely," he said. "You're going to have to go down to the Nuggets' Palace to practice marching."

"I bet Heidi can do it, too, if she doesn't compete, can't she?" asked Ti An.

"Pul-leese," said Becky. "I can't imagine anything more humiliating. I'm sure Heidi isn't going to be within a mile of that Challenge Cup."

"You don't know what Heidi's feeling," said Lauren with her hands on her hips.

I sighed. I got up off the bench and walked over to Patrick. "Okay, okay," I said, "enough of this reverse-psychology stuff. You just got them to volunteer because you thought it would make me want to enter."

Patrick shook his head. Dimitri walked up to him. Patrick handed him the piece of paper. "Wrong, Heidi," said Patrick.

"Vot's wrong?" asked Dimitri.

"Nothing," said Patrick. "Heidi thinks we're trying to pressure her to enter."

"You can probably march in the parade with us if you don't compete," said Jodi. "Can't she, Dimitri?"

"Okay, okay, guys, you win," I said. "I want to compete."

Patrick gave me a puzzled look. "Heidi, come into my office for a minute. You, too, Dimitri."

"Just give me the papers to sign," I said. "I'll do it. You don't have to think of any more tricks."

"In my office," said Patrick. He sounded serious.

I went into Patrick's office. He sat behind his desk. Dimitri stood by the door.

"What's wrong?" I asked Patrick. "I said I'd do it."

"Nobody's playing any tricks on you," said Patrick. "Neither Dimitri nor I would do that. Now, maybe we should have talked to you before offering to have the Challenge Cup brought to Denver, but we had to move fast. I don't want you doing this for me or for anybody else."

"Come off it, Patrick," I said. "That little charade with the Pinecones was designed to make me want to do it."

"Vot's she talking about?" asked Dimitri.

"The Pinecones are going to be the pages," I said. "You arranged it."

Dimitri nodded. "It's fun for them. Vot's wrong vith that?"

I blinked. "Nothing," I muttered.

"Heidi, only you can decide what you want to do," said Patrick. "You won't disappoint anybody if you decide to hang it up."

"What do you mean, 'hang it up'?" I asked him.

"Come on, Heidi," said Patrick, gently. "You're smart. You know you can't wait forever if you want to compete internationally again."

"Dimitri?" I asked.

"Patrick's right," said Dimitri. He shrugged. "There're new girls coming along. Ve have to let the judges know you are again a vinner."

I bit my lip. "Okay," I said, "let's go for it. I mean it. I want to do it."

Patrick looked at me for a second.

"Great," he said. That's what I like about Patrick. He doesn't dither. He could have asked me again, "Are you sure?" but that's not Patrick's way.

"Give her the paper," he said to Dimitri. "Your mother has to sign the release form, and then we countersign it as your coaches."

I stuck out my tongue. "I wish I could just sign it myself," I said.

"Do you want us to talk to your mom?" offered Patrick.

"No," I said. "If I'm brave enough to compete, I've got to be brave enough to ask her to sign."

"That's the spirit," said Dimitri. "She give you trouble, I talk to her."

"No, no, Dimitri," I said quickly. "I'll do it." Dimitri was grinning at me. "Now what?" I asked him.

"Ve going to set them on their nose," he said.

"Uh, excuse me?" I asked him.

"I think Dimitri means that you're going to make the gymnastics world sit up and take notice."

Dimitri just grinned.

8

Who Do You Trust?

"It's not a good idea," said Mom. She folded the paper neatly. We were in Dr. Joe's office. I had been smart about that. I had waited until one of our "family therapy" sessions. I knew I'd need all the help I could get.

"I didn't ask you if you thought it was a good idea," I said. "I told you that I'd decided I want to compete."

"Heidi," said my father. "I don't like you speaking like that to your mother." He looked at Dr. Joe. "Isn't it your job to tell her what's best for her?"

Dr. Joe shook his head. "No, my job is to help her figure that out for herself."

"Well, she tried and she almost killed herself,"

said my father. "We're willing to take our responsibility — maybe we pushed her too hard."

"Maybe not," said Dr. Joe. "Maybe Heidi's illness doesn't have its roots in gymnastics."

"What's *that* mumbo jumbo supposed to mean?" muttered my father.

"It means that *I'm* going to decide what I want to do, not you," I snapped.

"I do *not* like your tone of voice," said my mother. I felt like slamming my fist through the glass wall of the aquarium. I squirmed in my seat.

"This isn't about tone of voice," I argued. "It's about you trusting me. Isn't it, Dr. Joe?"

Dr. Joe nodded. "Maybe you should explain to your parents why you want to compete so soon."

Mom didn't give me time to talk. "Heidi, Heidi," she said. "I just don't want to see you getting hurt again."

"I didn't *get* hurt, Mom. I hurt myself." Suddenly I was yelling.

"Heidi, do not yell at your mother," said Dad.

Luckily I was sitting in a swivel chair. I spun around and stared at the aquarium.

"Heidi," said Dr. Joe, "turn around and face your parents."

"Why?" I muttered. "They don't listen."

"You haven't tried to make them hear you," said Dr. Joe.

I wanted to run out of there. Slowly I swiveled around. I couldn't find any words. I just stared at my parents.

Dad closed his eyes. "We always dreamed of your making the Olympics," he said. "But then when you got sick . . ."

"Mom, Dad," I said finally, "don't you see? If I don't at least try, I'll spend the rest of my life wondering if it's only because I chickened out."

"This is all nonsense that that fool Patrick has put into your head," snapped Mom. "If you were working out at a proper gym with a proper coach, it would be different. Patrick's a nobody, and Dimitri Vickorskoff — he's famous for being a loose cannon. These are the coaches she puts her trust in."

"Heidi's the only one who has to trust them," said Dr. Joe.

"She's a child. She's only fourteen," said Mom. "She doesn't know whom to trust."

"Heidi?" asked Dr. Joe. "What do you have to say about that?"

Sometimes I hate these sessions with all their stupid questions.

"About what?" I asked. I had already forgotten the question.

"Who do you trust?" Dr. Joe asked.

"Do I have to answer that?" I burst out.

"No," said Dr. Joe, "but try."

I sighed. "Mom, Dad, you've got to trust me on this. I know I'm ready to try a comeback."

"But what . . . what if the pressure gets to you and you stop eating or stuff yourself and make yourself throw up again?" asked Mom. "It could happen. Tell her!" Mom pleaded with Dr. Joe.

"Sure it could happen, but it won't be the end of the world. Heidi knows she's not perfect. She could slip, but I trust Heidi that she'd tell me or you."

I looked at Dr. Joe. He was right. I did trust him, and I trusted Patrick and Dimitri and the Pinecones. Amazing — before I had hardly trusted anybody.

"Mom, Dad," I said, "trust me."

My mother signed the release form.

9

Hanging Out with the Pinecones

"*Hobbies*," read Lauren, as she looked over my shoulder. I was at home, filling out the publicity form for the Challenge Cup. The Pinecones had all come over after practice. Mostly the questions were straightforward: name, date, and place of birth, gymnastics coach, number of years in gymnastics, best result in national competition (I was a silver medalist), best result in international competition (Eighteenth in Osaka, Japan), favorite apparatus (beam and floor). I scribbled in the answers.

The publicity form asked for my height and weight. I wrote down *5'* and *93 pounds*. When I competed in Japan I weighed only seventy-nine pounds.

I scowled at the blank after *Hobbies*. "I don't have any hobbies. Who has time to do anything but gymnastics and schoolwork? *Gymnastics* is a hobby."

"If you were me, you could put down shopping," said Darlene. "Maybe you should put it down anyway."

"I hate to shop," I said.

"How about hanging out with the Pinecones?" said Jodi. "That's a good hobby."

I laughed. "I can just see what the TV commentators would do with that one."

"Why don't you put it down?" asked Lauren. "It'll make you sound like some kind of mystical nature kid."

I giggled. "It'll drive Nadia Malenovich crazy," I said. Nadia Malenovich is the current world champion from the Soviet Union. She's incredibly competitive, and she is always looking for an extra edge. She'll try everything. She speaks and reads English fluently, and I knew she would read my publicity piece.

I wrote down after *Hobbies: Hanging out with the Pinecones.*

"I wish we didn't have to wear those dorky baggy white outfits," said Darlene.

The Pinecones were fast discovering that there was nothing glamorous about being the pages who get to lead the gymnasts in and out.

My mother walked into the room. "Heidi," she said, "if you've finished with the form, I'll be glad to type it up for you."

"Don't worry, Mrs. Ferguson," said Lauren. "I'm a good typist. I can put it on the computer."

Mom frowned. She was used to filling out all my forms for me.

"Thank you, Lauren," she said formally, "but I like to do it. It gives me a chance to check for spelling mistakes. Heidi just never learned to spell, and her handwriting is atrocious."

"No prob," said Lauren. "I'll run it through the spell check."

I tried to hide the smile that was forming at the corners of my mouth. Mom did not want Lauren to type my forms for me. Mom wanted the control, and no way was Lauren giving it to her.

"I think we should come up with some cheers for Heidi," said Jodi.

Mom looked horrified. "I thought you girls were going to be the pages," she said.

"Mom's right," I said. "If you're on the floor as pages, you've got to be strictly neutral."

"You mean, we can't cheer, 'U-S-A! U-S-A!'?" said Cindi. "I always wanted to cheer like that."

"I hate that cheer," I said. "When I was in Japan, the Japanese cheered politely for everybody.

They didn't just cheer for the Japanese gymnasts."

"What about just cheering your name? Hei-di, Hei-di's the One!" shouted Ti An. Ti An is usually so quiet, but she's got a really piercing voice when she's excited.

"Puhl-leeze," I begged. "Thank goodness you guys won't be allowed in the stands."

"Are you nervous?" asked Ti An.

"Ti An," objected Cindi, "don't give Heidi any ideas."

"Well, what's wrong with asking?" pleaded Ti An.

"Nothing," I said. My mother was still in the room. I wished that she would leave me alone with my friends.

"I'm not nervous," I lied. I was not going to give Mom the satisfaction of knowing the truth.

Mom looked at me suspiciously. I was wound up, tightly.

Lauren took my scribbled notes for the publicity form and sat down at the computer. Her fingers flew across the keyboard. She didn't even have to look down at what she was typing.

"Mrs. Ferguson, do you get nervous when you watch Heidi perform?" asked Darlene.

"Not really," said Mom, but I knew she was lying, too.

"Honest?" asked Darlene. "My mom almost gets physically sick watching Dad, but she can't stay away. You should see her — she tries to look cool, because she knows everybody's looking at her — but I've got to remember to wear thick sweaters, 'cause sometimes her nails dig into my arm and — "

"Darlene . . ." said my mother. "I get the picture."

"I just think it's cool that you don't get nervous," said Darlene. "I mean, I know I'll be so nervous just watching Heidi that I'll probably drop the sign I'm supposed to carry."

My mother gave Darlene a tight little smile. Darlene and my brother, Chris, are more than good friends, and I don't think my mother is too pleased.

Lauren finished putting my publicity facts into the computer. She turned on the printer.

Mom grabbed the sheet before it was even completely through and ripped the bottom of it.

"Don't worry," said Lauren. "I can print another."

Mom read it through. She pressed her lips more and more tightly together.

"Heidi? Did you write this?" she asked.

"Of course," I said. "It's all accurate."

"What's this about hobbies?" asked Mom. "You always put down listening to music."

"Heidi doesn't listen to much music," said Ti An.

"I know," I said sighing, "but that's what gymnasts are supposed to put down. It shows we're very musical and love the dance part of gymnastics."

"Is this supposed to be funny?" Mom asked. " 'Hanging out with the Pinecones.' That's your hobby?"

"It's the truth," I said to Mom. "And it stays."

10

Let Her Worry

Finally the week of the Challenge Cup arrived. On Thursday the Evergreen Gymnastics Academy hosted a party for the gymnasts and their coaches. "I can't believe the size of those girls," whispered Darlene. "They're teeny-tiny." Darlene is only thirteen, but she's tall for her age.

Yang Li, the leading Chinese gymnast, didn't look any older than Ti An, who's only nine. "You can't tell me they're all thirteen and older," whispered Cindi, who's eleven. "They don't look it."

"I've heard rumors that they lie about their age," I said.

"That's awful," said Ti An. "I thought gymnasts wouldn't lie."

I shook my head. "Ti An, you haven't seen anything yet." I tried to smile as Nadia Malenovich came forward. Nadia is seventeen, but she's so thin that she looks younger, until you look closely at her face. She doesn't look like a child at all.

"Hei-dee," trilled Nadia, "you look so . . . so healthy!" she exclaimed.

I knew that there had been plenty of gossip about me. Some of the gymnasts thought I was so sick there was no way that I could make a comeback.

"Thanks," I said. Nadia came forward and grabbed my shoulders. She gave me a kiss on each cheek, the way so many of the European and Russian gymnasts do.

"You look wonderful, too, Nadia," I said. Actually, I thought she was wearing too much makeup. The blush on her cheekbones was too red, and she had on bright blue eye shadow that looked old-fashioned.

Dimitri came up to us and gave Nadia a kiss on each cheek.

"This is your gym?" Nadia asked, looking around at our old warehouse.

Dimitri nodded enthusiastically. "Yes, yes, everyone here very fresh." Dimitri waved to the Russian coach. They gave each other a bear hug.

"No one thought Dimitri Vickorskoff would end up in such a . . . little gym," said Nadia.

"We're not that little," I heard Lauren say. I realized that I hadn't introduced the Pinecones.

"Nadia," I said, "I'd like you to meet my friends who work out at this gym." I introduced them all.

"It's so exciting to have you here in Denver," said Darlene. "It's a great honor."

Nadia wasn't paying attention. She was looking around the gym to see who else was here who was more important.

She spotted Chie Watsuta from Japan and gave her a huge wave. Without even ackowledging Darlene or the other Pinecones she took off across the room.

"She's a piece of work," said Darlene.

"Imagine having the World Champion in our own gym," gushed Ashley.

"We have the next Olympic champion in our gym every day," said Lauren.

I shook my head, "That's a real long shot." The Pinecones were embarrassing me. They just did not have *any* idea how good these gymnasts were and how tough the competition was going to be.

"Nadia is so beautiful," said Ti An.

"Excuse me," I said. I walked over to the corner of the room. I hate parties. I never know what to say or do, and I felt that everybody was talking about me.

Nadia was standing in the middle of a big

group. She was smiling and laughing. She looked so self-assured, like a movie star.

Nadia waved to me. "Hei-dee," she sang out, "come, talk some more to us."

I walked over to the group. I could feel everybody's eyes on me.

"It is so good to see you again," said Yang Li. She gave a little giggle.

"It's good to be back," I said.

"Dimitri Vickorskoff wanted this match here so that you could compete even though you're just the wild card," said Nadia.

"Meow," whispered Yang Li. I laughed.

"I don't know if that's exactly why Dimitri wanted it here," I said. "He's excited about his new home."

"It's not so fancy," said Tatiana, Nadia's teammate.

"We've got a new weight room and a couple of foam pits," I said defensively. "It's not so shabby."

"Speaking of weight," said Nadia, "you've gained weight." She paused. "On you, looks good."

"Thank you," I said with a slight sarcastic smile.

Yang Li put her arm around my shoulders.

"You look fantastic," she said. "I'm worried about having to compete against you again."

"I wasn't much of a challenge a year ago in Osaka," I reminded her.

"You look much stronger now," said Chie.

Nadia had a frown on her pretty little overly made up face. She yawned. "I have jet lag," she said.

"Oh, that's too bad," I said. "I hope you get your beauty sleep."

Yang Li giggled again. I spotted Becky Dyson, talking to the Pinecones. I motioned for them to come over. "Who exactly are all those girls you introduced me to?" asked Nadia. "They look like gymnasts, but I don't know them before."

"Nadia," I said with a sigh, "you don't know every gymnast in the world."

Nadia looked a little surprised. It was as if the only gymnasts worth knowing were the ones that she knew personally.

"Becky Dyson, here, is one of the better gymnasts in our gym," I said, introducing them.

Nadia shook Becky's hand. "You are a native of Denver?" she asked.

Becky nodded happily. "Oh, yes, I was born right here in Colorado."

"Then perhaps you can help me," said Nadia. "Something I don't understand. 'Hanging out with Pinecones.' Is that a usual hobby for girls in Colorado?"

Becky looked mystified. She hated the Pinecones. "Excuse me? Hanging out with Pine-cones? Only doofusses would do that."

"Doofoosis?" asked Nadia.

Darlene stepped in. "Oh, yes, Nadia. The Pine-cones were an obscure Native American tribe that used to inhabit the Rocky Mountains. They were incredibly strong and were rumored to have mystical powers that they got from a secret cere-mony they performed with pinecones."

"What are you *talking* about?" demanded Becky.

"It's a form of meditation that Heidi's been doing," said Darlene. "It's a hobby, but it's very powerful. She gets inner strength from the mys-tical power of the pinecones."

Nadia narrowed her eyes and stared at me. I smiled to myself. Let her worry.

11

Stop Hearing the Music

The fun and games and parties were over. It was Friday, the twenty-eighth. The Challenge Cup was a three-day event. The women's artistic gymnastics started things off on Friday evening.

I hated the schedule. We had our preliminary event on Friday. Then the men performed on Saturday, so we had a whole day to wait. The finals wouldn't be until Sunday afternoon. It was a killer.

I don't like evening events. My natural energy is in the morning. I hate having to sit around all day to wait to perform. It only gives me time to get nervous.

Mom drove me downtown to the Nuggets' Palace. I had eaten a light lunch, and I wouldn't eat again until after the performance.

The Nuggets had had a basketball game the night before, so we hadn't been allowed to practice in the arena.

Usually at a big competition the gymnasts get to practice in the actual site the day before. Each arena feels different. It is always the same regulation apparatus, but a place either feels "right" or "wrong."

We went in through the players' entrance. The guard asked for my identification. I had a plastic pass with my picture on it that showed I was a competitor. I put it around my neck and instantly felt good, like I belonged. I remembered my first big competition and getting my first pass. I had been so timid.

I wasn't so timid anymore.

Mom started to go into the locker room with me. The guard stopped her. "This is for the competitors only," he said.

"Nonsense," said Mom. "I'm her mother."

Just then the Pinecones trooped into the Palace, each with a plastic card around her neck.

"Hi, Mrs. Ferguson," said Lauren cheerfully. She opened the door to the locker room.

"Where are you going?" demanded my mother.

"We have to get ready," said Lauren. "Isn't it cool to be here? I'll bet we're the shortest people ever to change in this locker room."

"I'll vouch for that," said the guard.

"These girls are not competitors," said my mother. "If I can't go into the locker room, they can't, either."

"Mother!"

"We've got passes, too, because we're pages," said Cindi. "We have to practice marching. We carry the signs. Because all the competitors don't speak English, we carry a little picture of a beam or vault."

"Why are you telling *her*?" asked Jodi. "She's seen more major gymnastics events than any of us. Haven't you, Mrs. Ferguson?"

Mom's lips were in a tight line. "I don't think you need the Pinecones to distract you at this time," she hissed at me.

I didn't have time for this nonsense. "I've got to change," I said to her. I pushed open the door of the locker room. It was far different from our locker room at the gym. It was carpeted in a deep royal-blue, and everything seemed built to the scale of giants. I could barely reach the hooks on the walls.

Nadia, Yang Li, and most of the other competitors had already changed. Nadia was wearing a geometric-print leotard with a cut-out back. It was very sophisticated.

Dimitri wanted me to wear bright orangy red. It's not a color I usually wear.

"Vhy hide?" Dimitri had asked me when I was choosing. "Ve show everybody, you back."

I had six identical bright red leotards. I put one on, making sure that I picked one I had worn before. I *never* wear a new leotard for a competition.

I could feel the saliva in my mouth drying up, a sure sign that I was nervous. The skin around my eyes was dry and tight, but I felt alert. There's a sense of energy just in getting ready for a big competition. It's a rush.

If someone met me for the first time on the day of a competition, they wouldn't like me. On the day of competition, I'm beyond intense. If I were a rocket, I'd be going into hyperspace.

Nadia put her hand on my arm. "Last night, I asked my coach to do research. He says he doesn't think there's a Native American tribe called Pinecones."

"Nadia," I explained, "they were almost wiped out by the U.S. cavalry but they survived. They're making a comeback."

Nadia gave me a puzzled look. Darlene giggled, but I didn't dare laugh.

Actually, I wasn't in the mood to play mind games with Nadia. I had plenty to worry about just for myself.

I went out into the arena. The banks of judges' tables were set up around each apparatus. The floor mats were on a raised platform in the middle of the arena. The beam was to the right where ordinarily one of the baskets would hang, but it had been taken down for the event. I looked up into the stands and could see the television cameras and the technicians checking the equipment. They were using the same television setup that they use to televise the Nuggets' basketball games.

Loud music was playing out of the speaker system.

"This is so exciting!" squealed Lauren. "We're going to march in to the theme from *Rocky*."

"That's so corny," said Darlene.

"Dimitri picked it," joked Jodi.

I barely heard the Pinecones' chatter.

I walked out into the middle of the floor. Nadia had already started stretching. Naturally she had picked the dead center of the floor so that the rest of us would have to do our exercises around her.

Yang Li must have already stretched out. She was doing quick flips, one after another, from one corner of the mats to the other. Her legs were perfectly tight and together as she whipped back and forth.

I ignored her and started my own stretches.

Dimitri was over by the parallel bars, checking

the equipment. One look at his face told me that he was wound as tight as I was.

I concentrated on the way my body felt as I stretched first my large muscle groups in my legs and then began to isolate smaller muscle groups.

I stopped hearing the music. I stopped seeing the television technicians. I was no longer "hanging out with the Pinecones." I was back in the main arena. I wanted to be relentless. I wanted to win.

12

A Real Battle

The competitors were asked to leave the arena. We huddled together in the staging area before the Grand Entrance March. A computer divided us randomly into three groups, so each of us would have a different rotation.

I'm very superstitious. I believe that there are omens in every meet. If I had been meant to win, I would have gotten the rotation that I wanted. I didn't.

I told Patrick that I didn't think I'd have a good night.

He laughed. "Right, you might as well pack up and go home." Patrick thought I was kidding. I wasn't.

Being in a major international match is a lot like trying to concentrate at a three-ring circus. Something is happening all over the arena. While you're doing your beam exercise, which has no music, you have to tune out the noise and cheering from the other apparatus.

I like to get beam over early. The chances of getting a low score are so great that I hate to have it hanging over me. But, just my luck, I had the floor exercise first, then vault, parallel bars, and finally beam. My beam routine would come just as I was exhausted.

On top of that, Nadia was in my group. She is famous for finding ways to annoy you. They aren't illegal — they are just designed to make you lose your concentration.

I pulled off my warm-up suit and handed it to Dimitri. "Of all the lousy luck," I muttered. Dimitri knew how much I hated the rotation I had been given.

"No, no . . . good luck," said Dimitri.

"He's right," said Patrick. "No one knows what to expect from you anymore. You're fantastic on floor."

"On floor, you so strong, you vow them!" said Dimitri.

I heard a trumpet fanfare from the loudspeaker system. "Ladies and gentlemen!"

boomed the announcer. "Denver is pleased to welcome the world's top gymnasts to the Challenge Cup."

"I'm so nervous," stammered Lauren. She and the other Pinecones were dressed in white warm-up suits. Lauren was carrying a sign with a square on it, that stood for the floor exercise. The Pinecones were jumping around like fleas on a mangy dog.

"Why are they jumping around so much?" asked Nadia, giving the Pinecones a disdainful look.

"What if I drop my sign?" asked Lauren. "Oh, Nadia, Heidi, I know you have a lot more to be nervous about, still . . ."

"I am not nervous," said Nadia. She turned her back on Lauren. She really did look stunning in her new leotard. I felt that my red leotard was almost garish.

"That girl is a fool," Nadia hissed to me.

"She's my friend," I protested. "It's the first time she's been to one of these meets." I did wish, however, that Lauren would stop fidgeting so much.

The judges marched out first. Then I heard the announcer say, "Ladies and gentlemen, let's have a huge round of applause for the athletes." Nadia's name was announced first. She stepped through the tunnel and out into the spotlight. She did a perfect double back flip right in front of the television cameras. The crowd went wild.

Every gymnast got a really nice round of applause. It didn't matter which country she was from. When they called my name, there was a roar from the crowd. I went out into the blinding lights, and the noise grew even more deafening.

I did a double flip and looked up into the stands. My mother and father were applauding politely in the first row, but in back of them Big Beef was standing up, circling his right arm in the air, leading the crowd around him in shouting "HEI-DEE! HEI-DEE!" It was downright embarrassing.

"Who's that huge man?" Nadia whispered to me, as the other gymnasts were announced.

"It's the father of one of the Pinecones," I said. "He's a football player."

"What are these Pinecones?! They're everywhere!" exploded Nadia. She sounded annoyed. I smiled to myself.

The judges took their seats. There were twenty-four in all. They each had a computer at their desk and a telephone in case there were any disagreements.

I did some warm-ups on the side. I did a handstand pirouette. I tried to block out the sounds of the crowd and the sight of the judges. I hadn't been in a major competition for so long, I had forgotten how noisy it was.

Dimitri and Patrick left me alone. I liked that. I needed to be alone. When I finished my warm-ups, Dimitri came up to me.

Nadia was about to do her floor exercise. "Don't vatch anybody!" Dimitri admonished me. "Just vorry about yourself. No vorry!"

I tried to follow Dimitri's advice, but I couldn't help watching Nadia. She did a terrific floor exercise, full of ballet moves and intricate tumbling. There was hardly any filler in it. She scored a 9.9. One judge even gave her a 10. No way was I going to beat that score.

I wished I had taken Dimitri's advice. I didn't watch the other gymnasts. I closed my eyes and went over my own routine again and again in my head, trying to visualize it, seeing myself doing the most difficult parts with no problem.

Then my name was called. Dimitri and Patrick quickly put chalk on all four corners of the floor to give me traction for my tumbling runs.

I saluted the judges and took my pose in the middle of the floor. My routine starts with a daring double back somersault. Dimitri wanted it as an announcement that Heidi Ferguson was back. I semi-botched it, landing with my shoulders too low and my feet wobbly. I had to take a giant step to steady myself. I knew that something would be deducted right from the start.

Somehow making a mistake at the beginning of my routine relaxed me. It took the pressure off. I pulled myself together. The rest of the routine flew by. For my second pass, I did a roundoff back handspring, a one-and-a-half twist, another handspring, another one-and-a-half twist, and finished with a punch-front flip. I was across the floor in the twinkling of an eye. I could hear the crowd cheer, and they were clapping rhythmically. Normally I don't hear the crowd, but this time I did.

When I finished, I was panting so hard, I didn't think I would ever catch my breath. I saluted the judges. I was a little bit dazed. It had felt strange. I had no idea how I had done. Dimitri caught me in a bear hug.

"Magnificent!" he shouted at me, above the cheers. I shook myself.

"I botched up the first pass," I said.

"No matter," said Dimitri. "Sometimes girls fall apart — not you!" Dimitri's eyes were shining.

We waited for the judges' scores. There was obviously a disagreement, because I could see two judges on opposite sides of the floor talking on the telephone to each other.

"Uh-oh," I said. "I wonder what's happening."

The judges hung up their phones. My scores flashed up on the electronic board. I had gotten a 9.85. It was better than I had expected. I wasn't that far behind Nadia. Dimitri punched his fist into the air.

"It's going to be a real battle," he said. He sounded overjoyed.

13

In Your Face

The evening was over except for the beam. Unbelievably I was in second place. My vault had gone better than I had ever imagined, as had my bar routine.

Nadia was still in the lead. She was .4 points ahead of me. That doesn't sound like much but, in gymnastics, it's the equivalent of four touchdowns.

"It's goood, it's goood," Dimitri kept repeating to me. "It's better to be behind now. Vhere ve vant to be."

Nadia was doing her final one-touch warm-up on the beam. One touch means that you have a full minute and thirty seconds on the beam unless you fall. If you fall, you have to give up your turn to the next competitor.

Nadia started with an incredible full somersault onto the beam. She landed her practice mount with a solid thud. She did her routine as if the beam were four feet wide, not four inches.

"The pressure's really getting to her," I whispered sarcastically to Dimitri and Patrick.

Patrick refused to pick up on the sarcasm. "This is just where we wanted you to be. You're close to the top, but nobody's looking to knock you off."

"Right," growled Dimitri. "All the pressure on Nadia." She completed her dismount with a perfect double twist and landed it perfectly.

"Sure . . . sure," I said.

Nadia moved out of the way to let me do my warm-up. She started practicing her beam routine on the floor mats right next to the beam.

I needed to practice my new flair move on this beam. Even though my beam work had been solid all week, I felt shaky about it tonight.

As I jumped for my mount, Nadia did a twisting move toward the beam. Out of the corner of my eye, I saw Nadia's legs flashing. I lost my concentration for that moment and fell off.

Nadia smiled as I had to give up my practice turn to one of the Romanian gymnasts.

"Nerves?" Nadia asked innocently. "Perhaps

you should try your Pinecone meditation, no?"

I found a space on the mats and tried to practice my beam routine without the beam, imagining a line in my head. But I couldn't really do the flair without the height of the real beam.

Dimitri came over to me. "Stop now," he muttered. "You rest."

I nodded grimly. Once again Nadia was first in our rotation on the beam. I didn't want to watch her, but I'm only human. Nadia did her spectacular somersault mount, and she landed it as cleanly as she had in practice. The crowd cheered her. She polished off her first pass, three back handsprings — bing-bing-bing. She knocked them off with inches to spare. Then she lifted her hands to do her compulsory turn. Nadia has been doing ballet since she was two. She never misses. Suddenly I couldn't believe it — she began to wobble as she came out of the turn. She fought to regain balance, her arms were flailing around, and the next thing she was on the mats on the floor.

Her face was red. She didn't even take the fifteen seconds to remount and regroup herself. She climbed back on the beam, but then when she did her dismount, a double somersault, her legs splayed too far apart. She landed with her feet wide, and then she fell to her knees.

She stood up and saluted the judges. I waited

for her score. All she got was a 9.2 and she didn't really deserve that. She sat down on the bench by herself, looking grim. Her coach started to go over and comfort her. Nadia toweled herself off and glared at her coach. He backed off and left her alone.

Dimitri came up to me. He was rubbing his hands together. He didn't have to say anything. I knew Nadia had given me the chance of a life-time to beat her. Dimitri was smart enough to keep his mouth shut. There was nothing he could say now that would help.

My stomach was doing flip-flops. My hands felt sweaty. I dipped them in the chalk bin and clapped off the loose chalk dust.

The judges indicated they were ready for me. I saluted them. My stag-leap mount was solid. Once I felt the beam under the balls of my feet, I felt rock-steady. I did my turns without a wob-ble. Nothing wrong so far. I leaped to the other end of the beam, a back flip without any teetering.

Now it was time for the Ferguson Flair. If I didn't flub it, I could take the lead away from Nadia. I took a breath. I dived toward the beam. The spectators gasped because they thought I was falling into the beam, chestfirst, but I arched my back and caught the beam with my hands. Immediately I went into the flair. The audience loved it. I could hear the cheers ringing in my ears. Then I did a front flip when everybody thought I would be exhausted. There was nothing left to do but nail my dismount. I took a deep breath. My dismount is a double somersault to the floor.

My feet landed tight together, the momentum almost brought me to my knees, but I fought the impulse to fall forward. The new strength in my legs from the weight machines helped. I did a deep *plié*, but I held on. I threw my arms over my head.

In your face, Nadia! I thought to myself.

14

I Want To Be Alone

That night I couldn't sleep. I hadn't gotten home until well after midnight. It was so unbelievable. Nadia hadn't spoken to me after the competition. I was now in the lead.

The Pinecones and Patrick and Dimitri were ecstatic. I could have cursed the promoter who had designed the exhibition. They had wanted suspense. Nobody had thought of the emotional toll it would take on us. I had two nights to thrash through before the end of the competition.

I didn't get out of bed. I didn't want my parents to know I was awake. I just lay there and sweated.

Finally I could see the sky was turning light. I stayed in bed as long as I could.

My mother was already up. I wondered if she had had trouble sleeping, too. She hugged me. "Heidi, I'm so proud of you," she gushed. "It's like a dream come true. I knew you could come back. I just knew it."

I smiled at her. I could have said something nasty. I knew that Mom *hadn't* believed that I could make a comeback. But it seemed kind of petty to rub her nose in it now.

"What do you want to do today?" Mom asked. "Dimitri thought you should just rest all day."

"I want to go to the gym and practice," I said.

Mom frowned. "Dimitri said . . ." she started to argue. One look at my face and she stopped. Suddenly now that I was on top, Dimitri was a guru who could do no wrong. When she had been afraid, Dimitri was the one who had been pushing me too far.

I shook my head. My mom just didn't seem capable of thinking for herself.

"I'm going to the gym," I said. "Will you drive me, or do you want me to take the bus?"

"Take the bus?" Mom practically shrieked. "Why would you take the bus? Are you crazy? You were on television just last night. You're being silly."

I would be climbing the walls if I stayed in the house one minute longer. "I'm going to the gym," I said through clenched teeth.

"Okay, okay," said Mom. "What about breakfast?"

I knew it would cause a fuss if I didn't eat. "Sure," I said. "I'll just have cold cereal. I'll have lunch with the Pinecones at the gym."

Mom frowned again, but she let me get my cereal. I made a big deal of peeling and cutting a banana to eat with my bran flakes. Then when Mom's back was turned, I dumped the cereal down the disposal. I pretended to be eating the last spoonful and then washed my bowl and ran the disposal.

There was no way that I could eat a bite. My stomach was as tight as a drum.

Mom drove me to the gym. I felt more relaxed as we drove closer to the gym. The parking lot at the mall was nearly empty. It was too early for shoppers.

I walked into the gym. The Pinecones were there. Patrick had called a regular practice. He hadn't wanted their routines to be changed because of the Challenge Cup.

Darlene was up on the beam with Dimitri spotting her. He had recently begun to teach her a new routine.

Dimitri looked surprised to see me. Darlene stopped what she was doing. "And wot," she asked, in her best *Lifestyles of the Rich and Famous* imitation, "does the beautiful and victorious Heidi Ferguson do on her day off?"

Jodi picked up the refrain. "She comes back to see her old chums at the Evergreen Gymnastics Academy."

"Cool it," I snapped, but it was too late. The entire gym started chanting "HEI-DI, HEI-DI, HEI-DI!"

I waved my hands in the air a little helplessly.

Patrick was grinning. "Hey, I thought we gave you a day off to rest."

"I'll bet Nadia's spitting nails this morning," said Darlene. "She looked so mad."

Dimitri came over to me and gave me another of his bear hugs, only this time it made me feel like I was suffocating.

"So how are you?" he asked anxiously. "No aches, no pains? Vinning feels good, no?"

I didn't answer. So far "vinning" had felt *no* good.

Dimitri ignored the fact that I hadn't answered his questions. "That Nadia, she's a scared rabbit today. She doesn't know vot happened last night."

"Neither do I," I said quietly.

"Boom, boom, boom, you showed them all," said Dimitri happily.

Darlene stepped down from the beam. Cindi was looking at me strangely and not saying anything.

"What are you staring at?" I asked her.

"Nothing," said Cindi. "I just wanted to see if you looked different after winning."

"And do I?" I asked. "I haven't won yet, remember."

"You look kind of sad," Cindi said honestly.

I turned away from her. I started to strip off my sweatsuit down to my leotard.

"Vot you doing?" asked Dimitri.

"I need to work out," I said.

"I don't think it's such a good idea," said Dimitri. "I vant you fresh for Sunday. You be fresher if you rest."

"I don't feel like resting," I said through gritted teeth.

"Okay, okay," said Dimitri. "You do some slow stretches. . . . 'Nice and easy,' old Sinatra tune."

I rolled my eyes. I didn't want to do slow, easy stretches. I wanted to kick the walls down.

Suddenly I grabbed my sweatshirt and put it back on. "Vot's going on?" Dimitri asked me.

"Uh, I decided you were right," I said. "I need to relax. I'm going to the mall to just hang out."

"Goood," said Dimitri. "Take your mind on vacation today. Tomorrow sharper than ever. It's goood."

"Yeah, yeah," I said quickly. "I'm out of here."

I heard some whispering behind me.

I was almost at the door when I heard Darlene's voice shouting for me to wait.

I didn't want to stop, but I did. "What?" I asked impatiently.

All the Pinecones were suddenly standing near me by the door. "Heidi, are you okay?" Lauren asked me.

"Of course," I said. "I'm ahead, aren't I? Why shouldn't I be okay?"

"I don't know," said Lauren hesitantly. "You don't seem yourself."

"Do you want us to come with you?" Darlene asked. "I'm sure Dimitri and Patrick will let us."

"No," I said, louder than I intended. "I want to be alone, okay?"

"Okay," said Darlene, but she still looked worried.

15

Three Hundred and Twenty-Four French Fries

I sat in the fast-food arcade on the second floor of the mall. It had begun to fill up with shoppers.

A paper cup of papaya juice stood in front of me. I had bought it at the health-food stand. In my lap, I had hidden the nine containers of french fries I had gobbled up. I had eaten exactly three hundred and twenty-three french fries in less than an hour. I hadn't gone on a binge like that for more than a year.

A little girl came up to me. She was about seven years old. I tried to ignore her. She stood right next to me.

"Excuse me," she said. She had a glossy program with a picture of Nadia on the cover. I turned away. I couldn't bear to have anybody recognize me.

"Aren't you Heidi Ferguson?" she asked. "I think I saw you last night."

"Never heard of her," I muttered. The girl walked away, looking a little confused. I was more than a little confused myself. I looked down in my lap. I had one french fry left. I popped it into my mouth. Three hundred and twenty-four.

"Excuse me," said the high-pitched voice, again. I couldn't believe that little pest was back.

"Please go away," I said.

"If you aren't Heidi Ferguson, who are you?" asked a deeper voice. I twirled around.

Lauren, Darlene, Cindi, Jodi, and Ti An were standing behind me. It was Lauren who had spoken.

Very quickly, I put my hands in my lap and shoved the greasy paper cartons onto the floor. I pushed them away with my feet.

"What are you doing here?" I asked them. I wanted them to go away.

"We came to look for you," said Darlene, taking a seat. She looked under the table and saw all the garbage and frowned.

Cindi sat down next to me. "You don't look good," she said.

"I'm fine," I said, covering my mouth with my

hand. My shoulders went up as I belched. "You guys should be at practice."

"We got Dimitri to let us come look for you," said Darlene.

"That wasn't necessary," I snapped.

"Yes, it was," said Ti An, seriously. "Darlene knew something wasn't quite right with you."

"What are you, a great detective?" I asked Darlene.

Darlene shook her head. "I know that you hate shopping," she said. "I might go to the mall to relax, but not you."

"So what?" I asked. "I'm just sitting here, having a papaya juice." I held up my cup. The pulpy substance in the bottom of the cup was making me sick to my stomach. My hand was shaking. I wanted those three hundred and twenty-four french fries *out* of me!

I pushed away from the table and ran for the ladies' room. It was all the way down at the other end of the mall. It felt like a mile away. I sprinted. People coming toward me took one look at my face and got out of my way.

The Pinecones thundered after me, but they were no match for my speed.

I got to the bathroom and locked the door to the stall. I stuck my finger down my throat, deep down, past the flap at the back of my tongue, and made myself throw up. It wasn't so hard. It was something I had perfected a year ago. I flushed the toilet, then rested my head against the cool metal of the wall.

"Heidi?" I heard Darlene call. I sat on the toilet and pulled my legs up on the seat so they wouldn't be able to look underneath and see me.

"Heidi?" repeated Lauren. "Are you okay?"

"She runs so fast," said Ti An, sounding out of breath.

"What do you think?" asked Cindi. "She's a world champion."

I looked down. Lauren was crawling on the floor, looking under each door.

A few stalls down from me, I heard a lady scream.

"Whoops, sorry," said Lauren quickly. I burped. I couldn't help myself.

"Heidi?" repeated Lauren.

Slowly I opened the door. My face was all sweaty and clammy. I went over to the sink. I let the cold water run over my hands. I cupped them and splashed the water on my face. Darlene pulled down a paper towel and gave it to me.

I poured cold water on the towel and patted my face. Then I turned to them.

They looked horrified. "You look green," whispered Ti An.

"What did you do to yourself?" asked Cindi. Lauren and Darlene were silent. I knew *they* knew what I had done to myself.

"Okay, good!" I shouted at them. "I ate three hundred and twenty-four french fries and made myself throw up. Go tell Dimitri and Patrick. Tell them I ruined my chances for tomorrow! Go on — tell on me!"

The woman who'd been in the stall next to me gave me a disgusted look and rushed out of the ladies' room.

The Pinecones didn't look like they were going anywhere.

16

Please Don't
Mention Chicken

"Three hundred and twenty-four french fries!" exclaimed Cindi. "You counted them?"

"It's a good thing you kept it under three hundred and twenty-five," said Lauren.

Cindi stared at her. "How can you make a joke at a time like this?" she yelled.

I poured some more cold water over my face.

"It's a proven fact," said Lauren, "that anything under three hundred and twenty-five french fries isn't lethal."

"Lauren," protested Cindi, "stop kidding Heidi about this. It isn't funny."

"I don't know," said Darlene, leaning against the sink. "I kind of think it is funny."

I pushed Darlene out of the way and got another paper towel. "Very cute," I said. "But you know as well as I do that it was *sick* of me to eat like that. There's no way that I can perform tomorrow."

Lauren shook her head. "Not true," she insisted. "You stopped short of a fatal number!"

"Lauren," I shouted at her, "cut it out! This isn't a joke."

"I know," said Lauren, sounding miserable. "Why did you do it?"

"I couldn't help myself," I said. "I guess I'm just not as cured as I thought."

Darlene grabbed my arm between my shoulder and elbow. "What you're doing won't work, either," she said.

"What do you think *you're* doing?" I asked Darlene, staring at her hand on my arm.

"We're hanging out," said Darlene. "Isn't that what you listed as your favorite hobby?"

"Just a bunch of Pinecones hanging out in bathrooms in the mall," said Lauren.

This wasn't the reaction I had expected. I had expected the Pinecones to be horrified and to treat what had happened to me as a tragedy. The last thing I had expected from them was jokes.

"Don't you realize what I just did to myself?" I said. "I pigged out and then made myself sick. I can't go through with the Challenge Cup."

"That's in your head," said Lauren. "You're not really that sick. You're just looking for an excuse."

"Are you kids crazy?" I yelled at them. "I just backslid right down the path that landed me in the hospital. I did it to myself."

"I did something similar once," said Cindi. "Remember when I was scared to do the Eagle on the bars? I just about peed in my pants."

"Very nice image, Cindi," said Darlene.

"I threw up before our first meet," said Ti An. "And I always used to fall off when it counted."

"Used to?" asked Lauren. "You still do it sometimes."

"You girls," I said. "You're just Pinecones. You think the Atomic Amazons are big competition. You don't know anything about what it's like to be against the best."

"We know what you're like," said Lauren, angrily. "And don't put us down. You're just human and scared and you ate too many french fries and you threw up. So what? That doesn't mean you can't perform tomorrow, unless you're too chicken."

I took a deep breath. Lauren looked at me. I was older, stronger, and in some ways I was Lauren's idol, but she wasn't afraid to stand up to me. I thought about Dr. Joe telling me that it wouldn't be the end of the world if I backslid.

It would have been so easy for the Pinecones to pity me, but they didn't.

"So the pressure got to you," said Darlene. "I still don't think that means that you should just give up."

"You don't know what the pressure feels like," I said with a sigh.

"I'm still trying to imagine what it feels like to eat three hundred and twenty-four french fries," said Lauren. "Talk about pressure."

I did a double take. I couldn't believe that Lauren could still joke about this. Then I started laughing.

"You guys are too much," I said. "Maybe I was feeling a little sorry for myself."

"Yeah," said Cindi. "It's tough at the top."

"It is," I protested.

"Would you want to trade places with Nadia or any of the others?" asked Darlene. "I'm sure if you drop out Nadia will not be heartbroken."

"So you think I should just forget what I did to myself?" I asked.

"Maybe you should talk to your shrink about it," Darlene suggested.

"You're right," I said. "But *after* the match."

"Does that mean you're going through with it?" asked Ti An, excitedly.

"Yup," I said. "Do me a favor. Don't tell anybody

about what went on here. I'll talk to Dr. Joe myself."

"Sure," said Lauren. "I knew you weren't chicken."

"Do me a favor, please?"

"Don't worry," said Darlene. "We promise not to tell anybody."

"That's not it," I said. "I admit I was chicken. Just please — don't mention food to me again."

17

Beat the Pants off Her

On Sunday, I woke up feeling pretty awful. My throat felt scratchy from when I had made myself throw up. I got out of bed and brushed my teeth — that made me feel a little better.

I went downstairs and faked how I felt. I managed to eat a little breakfast and to keep it down. I was so glad that the finals were in the afternoon, not the evening.

"Are you okay?" Mom asked suspiciously.

"I'm fine," I said.

"You do look pale," said my father.

"I am fine," I repeated, enunciating every syllable. Mom and Dad looked at each other.

"Really," I promised them, "it's just nerves. I'll be okay once we get going." Mom gave me a funny look. She went into the other room, and I heard her make a couple of phone calls. I didn't pay any attention to her words. I was too nervous.

Later that morning, Mom and Dad both drove me to the Nuggets' Palace. Dimitri saw me first. He was talking to the Chinese coach, but he broke off the conversation when he saw me.

"Are you okay?" he asked me.

I was getting annoyed. "Is this today's password?" I asked him. "Of course, I'm okay. Why shouldn't I be okay?"

"You vere tall strung yesterday," said Dimitri.

I stared at him, then I figured out that he had meant to say "high strung."

"Just a little nerves," I said. I wondered if I should have brought a tape recorder with me that kept repeating "I'm okay."

I went into the locker room. Nadia was there. She gave me a dirty look. I put on one of my leotards and didn't bother to speak to her.

I went back out to the practice area. I looked up and my mouth fell open. Dr. Joe was talking to Dimitri, Patrick, and my mother and father.

I looked around for the Pinecones. I was furious at them. Had they gone back on their word and told on me? What other reason could there be for Dr. Joe to be here?

I couldn't see Lauren or Darlene or any of the Pinecones. I stomped up to Dr. Joe. "What are you doing here?" I demanded. "I feel fine now. I only ate three hundred and twenty-four french fries. I admit I made myself throw them up, but still the Pinecones had no right to call you."

Mom looked horrified. "Oh, Heidi, no . . . not again," she moaned.

Dimitri and Patrick were staring at me as if french fries were growing out of my hair. "Is there somewhere private we can go?" Dr. Joe asked Dimitri.

Dimitri nodded. He herded us to the trainers' room and closed the door behind us.

"Oh, Heidi, Heidi," wailed my mother. "I knew you didn't look right. I called Dr. Joe. I thought maybe you'd want him here today."

"You mean, the Pinecones didn't call you?" I asked Dr. Joe.

"Let's start at the beginning," said Dr. Joe. "Nobody called me but your mother. She was just worried about you."

"And with good reason!" shrieked Mother. "Did you hear what she did to herself?"

"Three hundred and twenty-four french fries — that's quite a few," said Dr. Joe.

"Lauren said that three hundred twenty-five would be really sick," I said. "The Pinecones said that three hundred twenty-four wasn't lethal."

Dr. Joe laughed.

"How could she make jokes at a moment like

this?" said my mother. She turned on Dr. Joe and Dimitri and Patrick. "That's it. It's clear that Heidi should withdraw from the competition. She's too fragile. She's started to backslide. Who knows where it'll lead?"

Dr. Joe ignored my mother. "How do you feel today?" he asked me.

"Okay," I said. "I'm thinking of making a tape recording that says 'I'm okay.' "

"Are you really okay?" Patrick asked.

I nodded.

"I'm sorry, Dr. Joe," I said.

"You don't have to apologize to me," said Dr. Joe. He hopped up onto the trainer's table. I don't think that Dr. Joe likes to think standing up. "Why do you think you did it?" he asked.

"Please," I begged. "This isn't the time for a session. I've got to warm up. I have a major competition today."

"You can't be thinking of letting her compete," said my mother. "What if she winds up back in the hospital?"

"What do you want to do, Heidi?" Dr. Joe asked me.

"Of course she vants to compete," burst in Dimitri. "She's vinning, for goodness' sake. She's on top. Vhy shouldn't she vant to compete?"

"Heidi?" asked Dr. Joe. I knew that Dr. Joe

understood that yesterday I had been ready to blow it all. After all, he had warned me that it wasn't going to be clear sailing.

"I want to do more than compete," I said. "I want to win."

Dimitri clapped his hands together.

"But . . . but," stammered my mother, "you could be too weak from your ordeal yesterday!" She turned to Dr. Joe. "Aren't you going to tell her that she can't do it?"

My father spoke up. "Let Heidi decide," he said.

Mom stared at him. Dad winked at me. "Good luck, honey," he said. "I hope you beat the pants off her."

"That's it?" I asked Dr. Joe. "No big psychological explanation? No lecture?"

Dr. Joe shook his head. "We'll have plenty of time to talk after the competition. This isn't the end of anything. It's just the beginning."

I rolled my eyes.

"Corny, huh?" said Dr. Joe.

I nodded.

"Well, then," said Dr. Joe. "Let me repeat the wise words of your father."

Dad looked up surprised. He's not used to being called "wise."

"What were those?" asked Dad.

"Beat the pants off Nadia," said Dr. Joe.

18

Fight It Out for Real

The Pinecones were in the practice area, peeking out as the crowd started to file into the arena.

Lauren saw me first and ran over to me. "Are you okay?" she asked.

"I swear, if one more person asks me that this morning, I'll kill them."

"I guess you're okay," said Lauren. "You've got the energy to bite my head off."

"Sorry," I said, "I've just had a 'meeting' with my parents and Dr. Joe and Dimitri and Patrick. All just to find out if I'm okay."

"Do they know about yesterday?" asked Jodi.

I nodded. The Pinecones looked worried. "It *is* okay," I told them. "I know you didn't tell anybody. *I* told them. Dr. Joe said it was up to me if I felt well enough to compete. I do."

The Pinecones looked as if they were having a hard time accepting the fact that I really was okay. I didn't blame them. Yesterday must have scared them more than they let on.

"You know what my father said?" I asked them. "He said to beat the pants off Nadia."

I hadn't realized that Nadia was walking by at that moment. She glared at me when she heard her name. As good as her English was, I don't think she caught all my words. But she got the drift.

"Are you okay?" Nadia asked me. I knew that rumors had started flying as soon as Dimitri had herded us into the trainers' room.

"I'm fine," I said to Nadia.

Nadia tossed her head. "I hear that you are — how you say? — still frag-ile?"

I bent my arm at the elbow and made a fist. My bicep jumped up.

"Does that feel fragile to you, Nadia?" I asked.

Nadia turned her back to me. "Aren't you worried about making her angry?" Ti An asked me.

"I don't have to worry," I said. "I'm the one who's on top."

The trumpets sounded in the arena. It was time to fight it out for real.

19

No Trading Places

The theme song from *Rocky* was playing again. I was sick of it. I wished that gymnastics *was* more like boxing or football. Nadia and I might be archrivals, but we couldn't touch each other. Neither of us could ever just settle it once and for all with a knockout punch. Big Beef could win the game for his team with a terrific football block that allowed the winning touchdown. I guess that's the difference between opponents and competitors.

There was nothing Nadia or I could do to each other that would change the score. It was all up to the judges and to ourselves. If I made a mistake, she could win. If she made a mistake, I could win, but I couldn't *make* her make a mistake. I could only try harder myself.

"You vill fight out until the end," Dimitri said to me. He was right. Nadia did a perfect vault, and they gave her a perfect 10. I did a good vault, but I had to take a huge lunge as I landed. It happened the second time, too. I didn't fall, but I gave Nadia an opening to narrow my lead.

On the beam, I was almost as good as I was on Friday night. The Ferguson Flair was perfect, but I had too much energy going into my dismount, and I was forced to take an extra step. The judges gave me a high score, but not as high as I had gotten on Friday.

Nadia could smell blood. She did a flawless routine. It wasn't as hard as mine because it didn't have my Ferguson Flair, but the judges gave her the same score.

She had pulled to within a tenth of a point of me.

Nadia did her bar routine first. She wasn't perfect, but she was darned close. The judges gave her a 9.9.

Now it was my turn. If I conceded more than a tenth of a point, Nadia would draw even.

My mount was a half-twist to the high bar, and it was solid. I arched my body into a handstand above the high bar and held it for a beat. My new upper-body strength was coming in handy. Next came my trickiest move — a high release that involved clearing the bar with both legs. My knees bent slightly midway through.

I went through the rest of my routine without a hitch. I got a high jump for my twisting dismount, but my landing didn't quite stick. I had to take a backward hop.

Dimitri was waiting for me. "Pretty goood," he said to me, but we both knew that it wouldn't be good enough.

The crowd groaned when my score came up. I had gotten only a 9.8. Nadia and I were tied.

Now Nadia and I had to repeat our floor routines for the championship. "It's how it should be," said Dimitri. "The best against the best. She's the von who's vorried."

I didn't pay attention to Dimitri's words. I remembered his telling me the exact opposite on Friday. Words couldn't help me right now. I started to feel clammy again. I got a towel and wiped my face.

The Pinecones looked scared. I walked by them to get ready for my floor routine. "Relax," I said as I passed them. "The fate of the world isn't up for grabs."

Again Nadia went first. She didn't make any mistakes. She was a champion, and in the end champions always find a way to fight back. She got a 9.985.

Then it was my turn. It was all up to me. I

could still beat her if I was almost perfect.

I did my first tumbling pass. I didn't stumble. I wasn't *almost* perfect. I *was* perfect. I heard the crowd roar, but they seemed very far away. Everything was slowed down. I felt as if I had all the time in the world. Two-thirds of the way through my routine, and I still hadn't made any mistakes, not even a little one.

Every move was so important. When a routine is going great, the pressure not to make a mistake at the end becomes almost unbearable.

I had only my final tumbling pass left. I had a choice of doing a single or double layout to end it. If I went for the single, I'd be safe, and I'd probably win. But if I made the double layout and landed it, I knew I would win.

I took a deep breath and ran across the floor. I punched up high into the air, keeping my legs straight, and I went around once, twice. My legs were coming down too fast. I wasn't going to land right. I fought with all my strength to turn my body around. I got my legs underneath me. I landed on the mats with a thud. All the momentum was carrrying me forward. I stuck my arms behind me and somehow I kept my balance.

I heard the crowd screaming for me.

I waved to the crowd and smiled. That was a first. The old Heidi Ferguson was known for never smiling.

Dimitri and the Pinecones surrounded me with hugs. I couldn't believe it. The judges' scores flashed on the screen. I heard the crowd roar its approval. I had gotten a 9.995.

"The next time a ten," said Dimitri. I just grinned at him.

We waited while they rolled out the podiums for the award ceremonies. They were shaped like giant drums of different sizes. The largest one was placed in the middle. The judges marched out again to give the awards.

Then my name was announced. I walked to the highest podium and stood on it, listening to the cheers. The Pinecones were cheering along with everybody else. They didn't have to pretend to be neutral anymore. I accepted the huge silver bowl from the head judge. Another judge gave me a giant bouquet of flowers. I waved it over my head.

Then Nadia's name was called out for second place. She accepted her medal and then stood in front of my podium. I bent down to shake her hand.

As she leaned toward me, Nadia hissed, "It's easy to topple from the top. It's a long way to the Olympics in Barcelona."

I kissed her on each cheek.

Later, as I was showing my silver bowl to the Pinecones, they asked me what Nadia had said to me.

"She said, 'It's easy to topple from the top.' "

"I knew she reminded me of somebody," said Lauren. "It's Becky."

"Come off it," said Jodi. "Nadia is ten times as good as Becky."

"But their personalities are the same," protested Lauren.

I laughed. Somehow thinking of Nadia as Becky brought her down to size. Yet I knew what Nadia had said was true. It's one thing to get to the top, but staying there was something else. And it *was* a long road to the Olympics in Barcelona. Still, I wouldn't have traded places with anybody.

"Nadia doesn't know how tough you are," said Darlene.

I nodded my head. I was tough, but I didn't know if I was tough enough to stay on top. Still, I loved the fact that I was getting a chance to find out. I thought about the new move that Dimitri had taught me and variations of it that we could try. It might be a long way to the Olympics, but I had showed the world that I was back.

About the Author

Elizabeth Levy decided that the only way she could write about gymnastics was to try it herself. Besides taking classes, she is involved with a group of young gymnasts near her home in New York City, and enjoys following their progress.

Elizabeth Levy's other Apple Paperbacks are *A Different Twist, The Computer That Said Steal Me,* and all the other books in THE GYMNASTS series.

She likes visiting schools to give talks and meet her readers. Kids love her presentation's opening. Why? "I start with a cartwheel!" says Levy. "At least I try to."

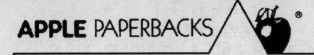

THE BABY-SITTERS CLUB®

by Ann M. Martin

Collect Them All!

The seven girls at Stoneybrook Middle School get into all kinds of adventures...with school, boys, and, of course, baby-sitting!

For a complete listing of all the Baby-sitter Club titles write to:
Customer Service at the address below.

Available wherever you buy books...or use this order form.

Scholastic Inc., P.O. Box 7502, 2931 E. McCarty Street, Jefferson City, MO 65102

Please send me the books I have checked above. I am enclosing $ _____ (please add $2.00 to cover shipping and handling). Send check or money order — no cash or C.O.D.s please.

Name _____

Address _____

City _____ State/Zip _____

Please allow four to six weeks for delivery. Offer good in U.S.A. only. Sorry, mail orders are not available to residents of Canada. Prices subject to change.   BSC790

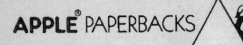